What You See Is What You Get

Adapted by Alice Alfonsi
Based on the series created by
Michael Poryes
Susan Sherman
Part One is based on the teleplay written
by Laura Perkins-Brittain.
Part Two is based on the teleplay written
by Michael Poryes & Susan Sherman.

Watch it on
Disney CHANNEL
abc Kids

Disney PRESS

VOLO

New York

Oscar® is a registered trademark of
the Academy of Motion Picture Arts and Sciences.

Printed in the United States of America

First Edition
1 3 5 7 9 10 8 6 4 2

Library of Congress Catalog Card Number on file.

ISBN: 0-7868-4639-9

For more Disney Press fun, visit www.disneybooks.com
Visit DisneyChannel.com

Part One

Chapter One

Bring it on, world! I'm ready for you! thought Raven Baxter as she strode through the halls of San Francisco's Bayside Junior High.

Her new pink lip gloss looked superfine with her pink sweater and pink pants. Her jet-black ponytail sat high on her head in a style that was totally smooth and sleek. And her hair band with the adorable purple flower perfectly matched her long suede jacket.

Awright! she thought, I am lookin' good in the neighborhood!

Singing to herself, Raven snapped her fingers to a song she'd heard that morning on the radio. Her best friend, Chelsea Daniels, was at home with a cold. So Raven kept an eye out for her other best friend, Eddie Thomas. She found him hanging out by their lockers. Walking over, she was about to ask, "What's up?" when she realized *nothing* was. *Absolutely* nothing. Her boy was standing still as a statue, staring into space—and, *uh*, drooling.

Okay, right, thought Raven. This could mean only one of two things: 1) Eddie needed a paramedic's attention, and quick, or 2) her best friend had floated up to that "Crystal daydream cloud" again.

Raven followed Eddie's stare—down the school hallway and straight into Crystal's pretty face. Well, thought Raven, at least I don't have to call 911.

"I know that stare," Raven said loudly into Eddie's ear. "That's the 'Crystal' stare, and *that* was the Crystal drool."

Gross. The boy had it *bad.*

Eddie shook himself free of the Crystal

cloud. "I don't know what you're talking about," he said, wiping his chin.

Obviously, her friend had come back down to Earth in total denial. "You've wanted to talk to that girl all year," Raven told him. "Why don't you just ask her to . . ."

Raven's mind ran through the possibilities: *Dinner* was out—it sounded too formal, and it could scare Crystal away. *The movies* weren't a great idea, either—you couldn't really get to know a person just staring up at a big screen for hours. Then Raven's eye caught sight of the banner hanging in the school hallway—that was it!

"Why don't you just ask her to the charity drive carnival this Saturday?" she suggested.

"I don't know, Rae," said Eddie, shaking his head.

"I know you're shy. It's okay," said Raven. "But I know a perfect way to get her to notice you."

"How?" Eddie asked.

In a deep voice, Raven shouted down the hall, "Yo, Crystal!"

Quickly, Raven wheeled away to face the wall of lockers. For a split second, Eddie froze. He could *not* believe Raven had just done that! In a panic, he spun away, too.

The hallway was crowded with students. So when Crystal looked up to see who had called her, she didn't notice Raven or Eddie. Both were looking way too busy opening their lockers. And since no one else stepped forward, Crystal just shrugged and walked away.

Raven turned to see her best friend hugging his locker tighter than a toddler with his favorite blankie.

"Eddie," snapped Raven, "I mean, if you're trying to date a *locker*, you got it goin' on."

Raven rolled her eyes. She knew Eddie was shy about making the first move. But she'd just given her boy the perfect opening—and he'd blown it!

A pep talk. That's what Eddie needed. But when Raven opened her mouth to give it, a powerful smell raced up her nostrils.

P.U.!

The odor was so foul, so *nasty* it jammed up her ability to speak—let alone think.

"Do you smell that?" asked Eddie, wrinkling his nose.

"Yeah," said Raven. She pinched her nose and waved her hand toward Eddie. "I was trying to be polite and not say nothin'."

"Now, you *know* that's not me," said Eddie, insulted.

The smell was not only nasty, Raven realized, it was *familiar*—and, sure enough, when she and Eddie turned to look, they saw a familiar face.

"Ben Sturky!" they cried together.

Raven could practically see Ben's body odor drifting off him in stinky waves as he strode down the hallway.

The kid had a grunge thing going, too—greasy hair, wrinkled cargo pants, and an old T-shirt with an open shirt and jacket tossed over it.

That was an all-right look if you were part of an underground garage band. But Ben took it too far. He didn't like to bathe. And he'd apparently never heard the word *deodorant*.

With his nose in a textbook, Ben obviously didn't notice the line of kids diving out of his way as he passed. When he walked by Eddie, he accidentally bumped into him.

"Sorry," Ben muttered as he continued down the hall.

Eddie looked horrified. Ben Sturky had actually *touched* him!

"Eww!" cried Eddie. "Does that guy ever

take a shower? Man, I've got second-hand stink here."

"Try having him in science," said Raven. "You know, my brother's hamster smells better—and it died two weeks ago!"

Eddie looked horrified again. "Cuddles died?"

Raven sighed. "He died the same way he lived—on the wheel."

Eddie nodded and continued talking, but Raven didn't hear him.

For a split second, Raven froze, and the whole world seemed to stop—

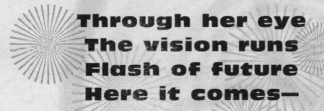

Through her eye
The vision runs
Flash of future
Here it comes—

I see my science class.

Sunlight is streaming through the tall windows. And there I am, sitting at my usual lab table, wearing my pink sweater and purple suede jacket.

I see Ben Sturky. He's walking up to me. Right up to me. No. No way! He's putting his arms around my neck. AHHH! Stinky Sturky is hugging me close!

Now he's saying something—

"This is gonna be great!" he cries.

When the vision ended, Raven felt sick. She turned to Eddie. "I just saw Ben Sturky put his arms around me."

Eddie grimaced. "Do your visions usually come true?" he asked.

Raven nodded, her eyes welling up. "Yeah," she said in a teensy-weensy terrified voice— but there was no time for tears or fears. The late bell was about to ring, and she had to get to class. *Science* class. Just like her vision!

When Raven arrived, her science teacher was standing near the doorway, handing out homework instructions as students entered.

"All right, class," Mrs. DePaulo announced, "your science projects are due on Monday, so I'm going to assign each of you a partner."

"Partners?" repeated Raven. She glanced across the science lab. In the sea of familiar faces, one fish stood out—one *stinky* fish, Ben Sturky.

Oh, no, thought Raven in a panic. Ben's going to be my partner! There's *got* to be a way to change my vision.

She turned to Mrs. DePaulo. "Do you really think having *partners* is a fair evaluation of our *individual* contributions to the world of science?" Raven asked. "I'm just sayin'."

The science teacher was no pushover. She

narrowed her eyes at Raven. "Yes, I do," she snapped. "And *I'm* just sayin'."

"Well, what about Diane?" suggested Raven, gesturing to her friend. "'Cause, you see, we have a chemistry—which must work well in science. I mean, *chemistry*, science, *chemistry*, science—"

"Diane's with Leland," Mrs. DePaulo said flatly.

"*Okay*," said Raven. "What about Tina? What about Christina? What about Robert—"

Before Raven could go through the entire class roster, Mrs. DePaulo cut her off. "Raven, I've already assigned partners."

"I know," said Raven, sighing in defeat. "Ben Sturky."

"Well, I had you with Kristen, but that's a much better idea," said Mrs. DePaulo brightly. "Ben," she called across the room, "you're with Raven."

Ben stared blankly for a second, taking in the news like a computer processing a new stream of data. Then his face broke into a goofy grin.

"Score!" Ben yelled. He raced over to Raven's lab table. "This is gonna be great!" he cried, hugging Raven tightly.

Oh, man, thought Raven, it's just like my vision. Only my vision didn't come with a noxious cloud of body odor. She actually felt dizzy.

"Partner," said Ben.

And Raven nearly passed out.

Chapter Two

Near the end of class, Mrs. DePaulo asked all of her students to pair up with their partners.

Ben shot toward Raven like a speeding bullet. In a super-excited voice, he began chattering—". . . and we're supposed to make a model of a molecule . . . but that's too easy. So . . ."

Raven gritted her teeth, nodded at Ben, and tipped back her chair, trying to avoid his body odor.

"I'm thinking an entire DNA strand," Ben continued.

Raven nodded again, and tipped back a little farther.

"So what do you say, partner?" cried Ben. "Let's get psyched! High fives!"

Suddenly, Ben lunged toward her, raising his arms.

Nooooooooooooo! thought Raven, not the *armpits*.

She tipped back so far this time, her chair went all the way over.

But Raven did have one happy thought before hitting the floor: maybe a concussion will get me out of this!

Unfortunately, Raven didn't get the concussion she'd hoped for. That meant she needed another plan.

By lunch period, she had one. It was a much better plan, too, because it didn't involve the emergency room—just the snack food machines.

"Oh, by the way," she told the table of

students, "the individually wrapped little brownies on your plates? Yes. That was provided by yours truly, *moi*." She laughed nervously as the kids eyed her with suspicion. "I *know* what you're thinking. I'm just trying to unload Stinky Sturky. I mean, Ben Stinky. Stinky Stinky—"

All the students rose from their chairs and left.

Man, thought Raven, just the *name* Ben Sturky could clear a table!

"You know, you could *at least* give back the brownies!" she shouted at their backs.

Uh-oh, thought Raven, I shouldn't have said that. She ducked as a half dozen little individually wrapped chocolate squares came flying at her.

Most of the brownies whizzed past. One fell on the table in front of her.

"This one's missing a bite!" she called

angrily. A second later, the brownie bite bounced off her forehead.

"Thank you."

Meanwhile, at another table across the lunchroom, Eddie was talking to his dream girl, Crystal.

"I've always thought you were so cute," he told her, "and, well, I'd love to go to the carnival with you."

Eddie watched Crystal lean toward him, her lips puckering. Eddie sighed and kissed her.

Just then, Eddie opened his eyes to find three boys staring at him, their mouths agape. Gulping, Eddie shook his head clear of the Crystal daydream—and lowered his sandwich, which he'd been kissing. Tangy tomato sauce dripped from his cheeks and chin.

"I just looove sloppy-joe day, y'all," he told the stunned boys. "That's all that is."

Just as they left, Raven rushed up. She opened her mouth to speak, then stopped, disgusted by the greasy mess all over Eddie's sloppy joe-kissing lips.

"Okay," said Raven, "I'm gonna need you to wipe that face before I talk to it."

Eddie rolled his eyes and grabbed a napkin. "Any luck finding a new partner?" he asked, cleaning himself up.

"No, and what am I going to do? This project's worth *twenty-five percent* of my grade. And I can't get a good grade if I can't breathe."

Ahhhhchooo!

Raven and Eddie froze at the sound of a loud sneeze. It was followed by the honking sound of a stuffy nose being blown.

"Head Cold Kenny," suggested Eddie, jerking his thumb at the table behind him. "He can't smell anything."

When Raven glanced over Eddie's shoulder,

her big brown eyes grew bigger. Kenny was sitting alone, surrounded by used tissues. His nose looked redder than Rudolph's.

This is my chance! Raven thought. She couldn't get over there fast enough.

"Hellooo, Kenny," she said sweetly.

Kenny had on a blue knit cap, and he was wearing, like, four layers of clothing. As he sipped chicken soup from his thermos, he listened politely to Raven's story.

When she had finished, Raven held her breath, waiting for his answer.

"Sure, I'll partner with Ben Sturky," said Kenny.

"You will? *Really?*" Raven asked in disbelief.

Kenny nodded and shrugged like it was no big deal.

But it was a *huge* deal to Raven. Kenny had just saved her nostrils, her sanity, and probably her grade.

Overcome with emotion, Raven suddenly knew how Halle felt when they gave her the Oscar!

"Okay, give me a moment," stammered Raven, tears welling up in her eyes. "I will be okay."

While Raven was talking to Kenny, Eddie was talking to *himself.*

"C'mon, Eddie," he murmured. "Get up. You can do it. Do it. Dooo it!"

Eddie stood up. Crystal was sitting only a few feet away. All he had to do was walk right over there and ask her to the carnival. How easy was that?

"Okay, I'm up," he told himself.

Suddenly, a girl walked up to Crystal and began talking to her. She was right in Eddie's way.

"Okay, I'm down," Eddie murmured, falling back into his seat.

Finally, the girl left and Eddie got up again. "I'm up. Cool," he said, then stopped again. "Zipper check." He glanced down. Whoops. "Okay. Close one," he mumbled, zipping up.

He stepped off again—right into a dropped pudding cup. The slippery mess sent him flying right into a kid who'd been walking along with his lunch tray. But it wasn't just any kid. This kid played fullback on the school's football team. Which meant he was a *really big* kid. And now he was a really ticked-off kid, too—because his lunch was on the floor.

The big kid picked up Eddie and tossed him like a bowling ball down Crystal's lunch table.

Eddie slid down the long table, finally slowing to a stop, his face in someone's lunch tray. He turned to discover it was *Crystal's*.

Not good.

So much for looking cool, thought Eddie. But what the heck. Hadn't Raven once told him that *trying* to look cool was the very thing that made some guys look *uncool* in the first place?

Besides, with his face in her lunch tray, at least he had her undivided attention!

After blowing off a piece of lettuce covering his mouth, Eddie smiled. "Soooo," he said, "want to go to the carnival?"

Eddie pretty much expected Crystal to blow him off. But she didn't. She smiled.

She actually smiled!

Fifteen minutes later, Eddie was dancing down the hall toward his next class.

"Want to go to the carnival?" he tossed to a group of girls. "Oops, sorry, I'm taken!"

"You could ask Crystal," he told a guy. "Oops, sorry, *she's* taken, too!"

He saw Raven, snapped his fingers, and pointed at her. "Yeah!" he cried.

Raven stared at him. "Eddie, you know you've got a piece of coleslaw on your head, right?"

Eddie reached up and found the wet, stringy piece of cabbage. "And I made it work for me," he told her, tossing it away.

"Yeah," said Raven shaking her head.

Suddenly, the whole world seemed to freeze in time—

**Through her eye
The vision runs
Flash of future
Here it comes—**

I see carnival day—
Wow! The gym looks great! Posters and balloons are everywhere, games of chance and refreshment stands are packed with people.
The whole school's here—

And there's Crystal. I see her with Eddie!

You did it, Eddie! You got Crystal on a date. You the man! . . . Uh-oh. Maybe not.

Crystal's making a face. A really strange face. Now she's pointing at Eddie's face and frowning.

"Gross!" she squeals.

When Raven came out of her vision, she saw a worried-looking Eddie staring at her.

"What'd you see?" he asked.

"Um. I just saw Crystal," she said. "And she was pointing at your face, and really grossed out."

"What's wrong with my face?" asked Eddie.

"Okay. Whatever it is, she's just going to freak." Raven didn't like delivering bad news to anyone—especially her best friend. But she had to warn him.

"What am I gonna do?" asked Eddie.

Just then, Raven and Eddie overheard a woman's voice. "It's straight to bed for you, young man."

They looked up to find Head Cold Kenny blowing his nose. His mother was walking him down the hall, her arm around his shoulders.

"With that fever, you'll be out for the rest of the week," Kenny's mother continued.

Kenny tossed Raven a stuffy-nosed "Dorry" as his mother hustled him toward the exit.

Raven turned to Eddie. "Dorry? That little stuffy head thing was my last hope!"

"Hey, partner!" called a voice from down the hall.

Raven didn't bother turning around to see who it was. She didn't have to. Ben Sturky's toxic fragrance was a better ID than a set of FBI fingerprints.

"Okay, you know what?" Raven told Eddie. "I'm just going to have to come clean. I'm going to have to be honest and tell Ben I can't work with him."

She didn't want to hurt the kid's feelings. But she herself was starting to *lose* feeling—in her nose!

Chapter Three

"Hey, Ben," called Raven, striding up to his locker.

"Oh, man," complained Ben, shifting his shoulders back and forth. "I think I must have pulled something in gym class."

Raven sighed. Whatever muscle this boy strained, she thought, he sure didn't strain it in the shower.

P.U.!

Ben began to stretch and bend. When Raven saw him lifting his arms over his head, she grimaced.

Armpits again? Oh, no, no, no!

"Hey, Ben. You know what might help that? If you keep your arms down by your sides.

Really tight." Raven grabbed his arms and slammed them down.

"Okay," continued Raven, "and you know what else might help that little arm spasm? If you take a really *loooong*, hot bath . . . with a big bar of soap. *Ooooo!*"

Ben nodded his head. "You know, that's a good idea. But actually this arm thing's kind of working," he said, pressing his arms even closer to his sides.

"So, what did you want?" he asked, stepping forward.

Raven stepped back. "Oh. Um. Well," she said, "I just wanted to talk to you."

"Is it about the project?" asked Ben, taking another step toward her.

Raven took *another* step back. "Yeah. I mean, I just cannot believe I'm partnered with you."

"Oh, I know," said Ben. "I still can't believe

I get to work with the prettiest girl in class."

"Oh." Raven stopped backing up. "That's so sweet. You didn't have to say that," she told him. "I mean, really."

"But I mean it," said Ben. "You're great!" Then he smiled at her—a big, goofy, puppy-dog smile.

Raven felt terrible. Here he was complimenting her when all she wanted to do was unload him. Well, she *couldn't* now . . . not like this.

"So," said Ben, "what did you want to talk about?"

"Um. You know, I just wanted to tell you that . . . uh . . . you're great, too," Raven fibbed.

"Awww." Ben raised his arms to hug her.

"Arms!" cried Raven, backing away. The boy not only smiled like a puppy dog but he *smelled* like one, too!

"Oh, right," said Ben. He lowered his arms to his sides again. Then he tossed Raven a final smile and walked off.

With a loud sigh, Raven collapsed against a locker. What was she going to do now?

"Do I sp-py a p-pupil with a p-problem?" asked Raven's English teacher, Mr. Lawler.

Mr. Lawler was a good teacher. But he had a small problem. Certain words surfed out of his mouth on a wave of saliva.

Raven had been hit three times in a row, and number four was coming at her—

"P-Perhaps I can help."

Dang! Her right eye got nailed.

"P-Possibly—"

Left eye, too!

"You know what?" cried Raven, trying to stop Niagara from falling again. "It's a science thing. And nothing you can *spray*, I mean, *say* would help. Sorry."

"Okay," said Mr. Lawler.

Raven began to exhale with relief when Lawler turned to walk away. "But may I p-propose you talk to your science teacher, Mrs. DeP-Paulo. Or is it DeP-Pallo? No, DeP-Paulo—"

The spit storm rained down again, and Raven grimaced. Man, she thought, if I'm gonna stay dry around Lawler, I'd better wear a raincoat and carry an umbrella!

"You know what?" Raven told Mr. Lawler, cutting off the shower. "We just call her 'Teach.' That's what we call her. And you know what? I'm about to go see 'Teach' right now. Buh-bye."

As Raven raced away, Mr. Lawler sighed to himself. "Teach," he muttered, "I wish I had a p-pet name."

The final P sent a saliva spray against the back of a passing student. The kid looked up at the sprinkler system, shook his head, then walked away.

Raven psyched herself up as she strode toward Mrs. DePaulo's science classroom.

Okay, girl, she told herself, this is your last shot. Mrs. DePaulo is tough, but you're tougher. Don't be a wimp now. Show some of that Baxter backbone and twist that woman around your little finger.

Raven barreled right into the empty room and stepped up to her teacher. "Mrs. DePaulo, do you have a minute?"

Mrs. DePaulo looked up from a pile of homework papers. "Raven!" she said with a big smile. "I've been meaning to talk to you. I am so *proud* of the way you've been working with Ben Sturky. A lot of students would have complained. But not you."

Raven bit her lip. "No."

"Now, what did you want to see me about?" the teacher asked.

"Yeah, okay, um . . ." Raven muttered. Her teacher had just sung her praises for being tolerant. How could she possibly complain about Ben now?

"Um . . ." Raven stalled. Just make something up, she told herself. "I was wondering . . . Is it *DePallo* or *DePaulo*?"

"DePaulo."

"Okay. I thought so!" Raven turned and walked away. So much for Baxter backbone!

Behind her, Mrs. DePaulo snickered to herself. "That was almost too easy," she murmured. In fact, if outsmarting students were an Olympic event, she'd get the gold medal every time.

But the teacher had spoken too soon. Raven had already stopped herself in the hallway, turned around, and marched right back in.

"Mrs. DePallo—"

"DePaulo," said the teacher, correcting Raven's pronunciation.

"Whatever!" cried Raven. "Ben stinks!"

Mrs. DePaulo frowned. "Isn't that a little harsh?"

"Ben's a nice guy—don't get me wrong," said Raven, "but ever since I was just a little tyke, I've been allergic to BO. All right? I don't go to sporting events, gyms . . . You know, you can ask my doctor."

"Well, this project is a big part of your grade," the teacher pointed out.

"And I really want to do well in it," said Raven. She meant it, too. She'd already convinced herself that working with Ben would be a disaster. And she just couldn't bear to watch her science grade go down in flames.

"Okay," said Mrs. DePaulo. "I won't force you to work with Ben. I'm very—"

Suddenly, Raven froze, and for a split second time seemed to stop.

**Through her eye
The vision runs
Flash of future
Here it comes—**

I see my science class again.

Ben and I are standing side by side in front of the room, and all the kids are staring at us—but not in a bad way. They actually all look impressed, like we did something great.

Ben is holding our science project—a DNA model. "We got an A," he says.

I can't believe it. An A? Awright!

With a big smile, Ben lifts the model high in the air. As his arms go up, his smelly armpits give off waves of stink, and the class

passes out. But Ben's still smiling, and so am I.
We did it! Oh, yeah! Ben's my boy. He may
reek, but that's okay. Because of him, I got
an A!

As Raven shook her head clear of the vision,
she heard Mrs. DePaulo say, ". . . and I'll just
have to tell Ben—"

"How much I am looking *forward* to working with him!" Raven quickly finished for her.

Her vision had given her a whole new attitude. If partnering with stink-boy meant an A
on this science project, well, maybe Ben didn't
smell *so* bad, after all.

"Did I tell you Ben's my boy?" said Raven.

Mrs. DePaulo scratched her head. "But I
thought he stinks."

"Now, Mrs. DePaulo," said Raven disap-
provingly, "that's a little *harsh*, don't you think?
Shame on you."

Chapter Four

Three days later, Raven and Ben were in the Baxters' living room, working hard on their DNA model.

"Hey, Ben," said Raven, sitting next to him on the couch. "Doesn't that go up there?"

Raven pointed to the top of the model, which was standing on the coffee table in front of them.

"Oh, yeah," said Ben.

"Yeah." Raven nodded.

As Ben reached his left hand up to place the piece on the model, Raven whipped out a bottle of her favorite perfume.

Spritz! Spritz!

She zapped Ben's stinky left armpit.

Got ya! she thought. And Ben hadn't even noticed. Before he turned around again, she hid the bottle behind her back.

"You know what?" she said. "There's something on the back of your head. You better get it."

"Yeah?" said Ben as he lifted his right hand to feel the back of his head.

Spritz! Spritz!

Yes! thought Raven. Right armpit nailed!

When Ben didn't feel anything on his head, he turned back to Raven.

"Oh," she said with a laugh. "It was just your hair!"

On the other side of the room, Raven's mother was coming down the stairs. Mrs. Baxter was pleased to see her daughter working so hard on a science project. But the satisfied smile on her face flatlined fast when Ben's body odor reached her nose.

Hit by the wall of stink, Mrs. Baxter turned her head, gulped a deep breath of fresh air, then crossed over to Ben.

"Looks great, keep up the good work, so glad to have you in the house, come again soon," Mrs. Baxter squeaked out fast without taking a breath.

"Oh, thanks, Mrs. Baxter," said Ben, as Raven's mother raced away.

"Mom," whispered Raven, following her mom to the kitchen door, "you gotta breathe sometime."

"Not in here," she whispered back.

As Mrs. Baxter ducked through the kitchen door, Raven's little brother Cory waltzed in wearing a diver's mask and snorkel.

"Hey, Cory, what's with the snorkel?" asked Ben. "How do you breathe?"

Cory removed the snorkel mouthpiece. "I don't. That's kinda the point," he said, then he jammed the mouthpiece back in and headed upstairs.

Ding-dong!

Raven was grateful for an excuse to avoid the couch. She opened the front door, and Eddie rushed in.

"I finally figured out what was so gross about me in your vision," Eddie told Raven. His orange turtleneck sweater was pulled up to cover his chin.

"What?" she asked.

"This!" Eddie pulled the turtleneck down to reveal—a flesh-colored Band-Aid.

Big deal, thought Raven. "You have a bandage!" she cried in mock horror.

"Covering a huge zit!" cried Eddie.

From the couch, Ben noticed Eddie and started to get up. "Hey, Eddie."

"Don't get up!" Eddie said in a panic. "You just keep working. Right *there.*"

Eddie turned to Raven. "Kitchen," he told her.

When they got to the kitchen, Raven's mother was still there. But Eddie didn't care. He was too upset to try to keep this zit problem private.

"I mean, why don't I just tell Crystal I cut myself shaving?" he asked Raven.

Raven rolled her eyes at her friend's baby-smooth cheeks. "Okay," she said, " 'cause if she believes that, you gotta dump the girl, 'cause she's kinda slow."

"Well, no, no," said Mrs. Baxter, walking over to Eddie. "He's got a little mustache coming on," she said, examining his upper lip. Then she frowned. "Oh, no, I'm sorry," she told Raven. "I'm thinking of your friend, Audrey."

Raven tried not to laugh, but Eddie caught her. "You think it's funny?" he said angrily. "You think *this*—is funny?"

He peeled off the Band-Aid.

Raven grimaced at the site of the erupting pimple. Mount Saint Helens wasn't as scary as that angry red thing on her friend's chin.

"Okay," said Raven, "I'm gonna need you to cover that back up."

Just then, Raven's father burst through the kitchen door, his arms filled with groceries—and his nostrils plugged up with tissue.

"I appreciate your concern, Ben," Mr. Baxter called back into the living room. "It's just a little nosebleed."

Then Mr. Baxter let the door swing shut and pointedly told Raven, "I need him out of my house."

"But we haven't finished our project," Raven complained.

"Here's an idea," said Raven's father as he put the groceries on the counter. "Why don't you work at *his* house?"

"No, no, no. Uh-uh," said Raven, horrified.

"I cannot do that. Because, you see, I've never met his family. He might be the *clean* one."

Mr. Baxter shook his head in disgust. Then he noticed Eddie.

"Ooh, Eddie, the Band-Aid on the zit trick. So, what did you do?" he asked, with a snicker. "'Cut yourself shaving?'" Mr. Baxter made quote marks in the air with his fingers, and Eddie felt like a complete idiot.

"That's it," Eddie said. "There's no way I'm going to the carnival tomorrow. I'm calling Crystal and saying I'm sick."

"No, you're not," said Raven. She pulled a facial steamer out of the cupboard and smacked it down on the counter. "See, what you're gonna do is stick your face in there, and it's gonna suck it all out."

Eddie eyed the plastic mask. It looked like some kind of torture device. "I'm not putting my face in *there*," he said with a shudder.

"But you don't have to," said Mr. Baxter. "Look, Crystal's not gonna care about that pimple. Sure, she'll see it. But then she'll spend some time with you, you'll make her laugh, and soon she'll want to know the man behind the pimple."

Mr. Baxter peeled back the Band-Aid on Eddie's chin. "Oh," he said, grimacing. "If she can *find* the man. 'Cause that thing is nasty."

Raven sighed. "You know, I found the best place to hide from them—

"In here!" she cried, and shoved his face into the plastic mask of the facial steamer.

For the next hour or so, Raven went back to work with Ben, and Mrs. Baxter took over working on Eddie.

When the steamer didn't work, she tried every spa treatment she could think of. She shoved his face in a bowl of ice water.

But that didn't work.

Waxing strips came next. *Zip-zip* went the strips.

Ow-yow! cried Eddie.

Finally, came the skin treatment. Mrs. Baxter had given Eddie her expensive "mud" mask. Eddie took the tube of gunk into the bathroom and smeared the green stuff all over his face. Within ten minutes, the whole thing hardened into a concrete mask.

"I can't move my face," said Eddie, walking back into the kitchen.

Mr. Baxter laughed. "That's because you were only supposed to put it here," he said, pointing to Eddie's chin.

Eddie tried, but he couldn't move one facial muscle. "Just so you know," he told Mr. Baxter, "I'm giving you a *really* dirty look right now."

After Eddie left to wash off his face, Raven walked in.

"Twenty-eight minutes and nineteen seconds," she said, gulping in great breaths of fresh, clean, stink-free air. "That's how long I, and my nose, have been in there. The good news: I've finished the project. The bad news: we have to burn the couch."

Unfortunately, Raven's little brother had taken the Great Stink Invasion to heart. Bursting into the kitchen with a towel tied around his neck in a superherolike cape, he shouted, "Have no fear, family! I'm going to *blow* the stink away."

He flipped a switch and the big electric leaf blower in his hands powered up.

The high-pitched screech of the machine sent Raven into a freeze-frame vision—

Through her eye
The vision runs
Flash of future
Here it comes—

I see our model—

Our beautiful DNA model is hanging in midair. The room's lamplight is glinting off its shiny glass surfaces. Then—

SMASH!

It hits the floor and shatters. Pieces fly everywhere!

AHHH! This is a disaster! My grade is sunk! I think.

Emerging from her vision, Raven lunged at her little brother.

"My project's gonna get ruined!" she cried. "I cannot let that happen!"

Raven tore the leaf blower from Cory's hands and turned it on him, blowing him backward. Then she shut off the machine, put it down, and raced toward the living room to protect her science project.

But as she swung the kitchen door, she felt

it strike something on the other side. An instant later she heard it—

Smash!

For a terrible moment, there was nothing but silence. Then Ben's voice called out weakly, "I'm okay. It's just the project."

Raven didn't want to look. She really didn't. But finally, she did. The DNA model was on the floor, smashed into itty-bitty pieces, just like her vision.

Ahhh! she thought. This is a *disaster*! My grade is sunk!

Ben patted Raven on the back. "We can fix it tomorrow after the carnival," he told her, reassuringly. "Even if it takes all night."

"All night?" Raven said in disbelief.

Raven felt faint. Mrs. Baxter started breathing through her mouth again. And Mr. Baxter just sighed. "I feel a nosebleed coming on," he said.

Chapter Five

The next day was carnival day. And the day of Eddie's big date with Crystal.

Colorful booths packed the school gym. There were games of chance, refreshment stands, and even a few amusement rides in the parking lot.

Raven was psyched. Almost everyone from school had come, and many had brought their families, too. Not only was the charity drive going to be a success, but she'd also found a way to de-stink Ben Sturky.

"Um, hey, Ben," she called up to her project partner, who was sitting above the carnival's dunk tank.

At the moment, he was sitting on a hinged

platform connected to a round metal target. Whenever a player hit the bull's-eye, the platform was supposed to collapse and Ben would get dunked.

Any minute now, thought Raven, this boy's going to have his first bath in recent history. Raven had secretly added detergent to the tank's water—enough to de-stink a skunk!

The plan was perfect, as long as someone actually *hit* the target. The carnival had been open for two hours already, and Ben was still as dry as the Sahara Desert.

If this boy *doesn't* get dunked today, thought Raven, I'm going to have to bring an oxygen tank to tonight's study session!

Raven gave Ben a big smile. "It's so great that you volunteered to help out with the dunk tank," she said.

Just then, a ball soared by, missing the bull's-eye.

Dang! thought Raven. That one was way off!

"Actually, you volunteered me," Ben reminded her.

Another ball soared by, again missing the target. Was this thrower blind? Raven thought.

"Oh, that's all right," Raven told Ben. "It's all for charity."

Yet another ball missed the target. And Raven couldn't believe it.

"Oh, come on!" she finally yelled, losing patience with the ball thrower. "You throw like a girl!"

Insulted, Raven's father frowned at his daughter, then turned and marched off in a huff.

Oops, thought Raven, guess I got a little carried away there.

* * *

While Raven was annoying her father at the dunk tank, her mother was bothering the barker at the basketball toss.

"Lady, could you give someone else a chance?" asked the man running the booth.

Mrs. Baxter looked outraged. "No! My baby wants it, and my baby's getting it!"

Cory grinned as his mother pointed to a big stuffed animal.

"That big spotted dog is coming down!" she cried and sunk another basket.

"You da man!" shouted Cory, dancing around his mom. "Go, Mama! Go, Mama! Go, Mama! Go! Go!"

A short time later, it was obvious to Cory that his mother had become caught up in some sort of game fever. Her arms were full of prizes, yet she still kept moving from game to game with a sort of wild look in her eyes.

As she picked up yet another stuffed-animal prize at the ringtoss game, Cory finally pointed to one of the stuffed animals. "Mom, can I have one of those?" he asked.

"No," said Mrs. Baxter, scanning the horizon for yet another game to win.

On their way to the horseshoe throw, Cory's father saw them. He pointed to one of the carnival's refreshment stands.

"Ooh," said Mr. Baxter, "nothing like a barbecue grill to get the juices flowing."

"No," said Mrs. Baxter, "I'm feeling lucky."

Cory shrugged and tagged along with his mother. Lucky or obsessed, he wasn't sure which his mother *really* was. But, hey, what did it matter? As long as she forked over a few of those prizes by the end of the day, either one worked for him!

Mr. Baxter, on the other hand, didn't care about the carnival games. The sweet smell of grilled meat had made him hungry. With a big smile on his face, he approached the barbecue booth.

The man at the grill looked up to wait on Mr. Baxter. It was Raven's saliva-spewing English teacher, Mr. Lawler.

"We've got p-piping hot p-pork ribs, hamburger p-patties, and soda p-pop," said the teacher, sending sizzling sprays of spittle all over the grilling meats.

No way, no how, thought Mr. Baxter. All of a sudden, he wasn't so hungry anymore!

"I'll have a root beer. With a lid," he told the teacher.

"P-Perfect!" said Mr. Lawler, spit flying into the drink—right before he placed the lid on it.

Oh, well, thought Mr. Baxter, it's all for charity. He took the drink, paid for it, then tossed it into the trash.

* * *

Meanwhile, over at the ringtoss game, Raven was actually having fun. She'd gotten two in a row, and she just needed one more to win.

"Hey, Raven?" called Crystal. "Have you seen Eddie?"

"You know what, Crystal?" said Raven. "I think he's over there by the cotton-candy machine."

"Okay, thanks," said Crystal.

"Okay, no problem," replied Raven.

Raven sighed, glanced down at the floor of the ringtoss booth, and whispered, "I cannot keep doing this."

Eddie sat up with the Band-Aid back on his chin. Hiding from Crystal was the only solution he could think of.

"Why not?" Eddie asked Raven.

"Because you told her you'd meet her here," Raven pointed out.

"And you told me this would be gone," he

said, pointing to his chin. "What am I gonna do, Rae?"

"You know what, Eddie, face it, okay? There's only one thing you *can* do," Raven said. She tossed the last ring. It missed. Sighing, she took Eddie by the hand and over to a secluded area behind the big dunk tank.

Fishing through her bag, she found her makeup kit and began to work, carefully covering Eddie's zit with dabs of cover-up cream.

"Yes," she told Eddie. "It is the magic of makeup."

"It's just so weird," said Eddie.

Raven handed Eddie her compact, and he looked into the small mirror.

"Hey, that's amazing!" he cried. "You can't even see it."

Then a thought occurred to Eddie. If

Raven's makeup could hide his blemish so easily, then what did she use it for?

"So, what do you *really* look like?" he asked, staring at his best friend suspiciously.

Raven shook her head. "You will never know," she said.

Then she pointed to the carnival floor. Time to find Crystal! Eddie nodded and headed out.

Raven was about to follow when she noticed Ben sitting on the dunk tank platform.

The boy is still high and dry! Raven realized in disgust. Couldn't anyone hit the darned target?

She watched as a line of players all took their turns.

A throw . . . and a miss.

A throw . . . and a miss.

A throw . . . and a really huge miss!

Raven couldn't take it anymore. "Can't you wimps hit anything?" she cried.

Suddenly, a dozen balls came flying right at Raven. And wouldn't you know it, most of those were direct hits!

Dang, she thought. I should really learn to keep my mouth shut.

Chapter Six

Eddie found Crystal by a refreshment stand. He bought them both hot pretzels with mustard, and they walked around, enjoying the carnival together.

"So, what's your favorite color?" asked Eddie.

"Well, it's between periwinkle blue and seafoam green," replied Crystal.

O-kay, thought Eddie. He didn't know what periwinkle was, but it sounded nice when Crystal said it. "Mine, too," he said quickly.

"Really?" asked Crystal.

"Yeah. We have a lot in common, girl," he said with a laugh.

Crystal laughed, too. They were really

having a good time together. Then she noticed Eddie still had a little mustard on the corner of his mouth.

"Oh, um . . . you've got a little mustard . . ."

"Well, let me knock that out, baby," he told her. With the paper napkin in his hand, Eddie carefully wiped around his mouth, trying to avoid his chin.

Crystal frowned. "Still there," she said. "You know what—"

Before Eddie could stop her, Crystal used her own napkin. As she wiped Eddie's mouth and chin, Raven's makeup came off on her napkin.

"Gross!" she cried, pointing at Eddie's chin.

Eddie felt terrible. It had all happened just like Raven had described it.

"All right," said Eddie, hanging his head. "It's disgusting. I know."

Crystal was too good for him, anyway,

he thought, walking away. The date was a mistake—and so was he.

"Eddie, get back here!" It was Raven. She'd seen what had happened, and she was boiling mad.

"Crystal, what is wrong with you?" demanded Raven, striding right up to the girl. "It is just a pimple. So what? Eddie is a great guy. If we let little stupid stuff like that get in the way, we'd never get to know anybody. I mean, look—"

Raven pointed to Mr. Lawler, at the barbecue grill. "He spits, but I know he's a great teacher."

Then she pointed to a classmate by the cotton-candy stand. "Look, she has a mouthful of braces, but she's also the fastest girl in track."

Finally, she pointed to Ben at the dunk tank. "And he smells, all right, but he's good in science and he's a nice guy . . ."

Raven's voice trailed off as she realized, really realized, that she meant what she was saying. "He's a nice guy . . . who deserves to be treated a lot better."

Here she was getting mad at Crystal for being superficial—when she herself had been doing the same thing to Ben.

"All for a stupid grade," murmured Raven, disgusted with herself. She walked off toward Ben. And Crystal walked up to Eddie.

"Look, Eddie, you know what?" Crystal said. "I don't care about a stupid pimple. It's just the makeup that's weird."

"Well, I only did it so that you would like me," said Eddie, looking at the floor.

"Eddie, I wouldn't have come here today if I didn't like you," she told him.

He looked up, into her eyes. "For real?"

"Yes." Crystal shook her head. "Can we just start over, maybe?"

"Well," said Eddie, looking away, "I've really got to think about this—" A split second was all it took. "Yes!" he told her with a big smile.

She smiled back.

Over at the dunk tank, Raven walked up to Ben.

"Hey," he said. "I'm still dry. Must be some kind of record here, huh?"

"Uh, Ben . . . could you please come on out of there?" Raven said. "I kinda need to talk to you about something."

"Sure. What's up?" he asked.

"Well, this is kinda hard to say—" Without thinking, Raven put out her hand to steady herself and accidentally leaned on the dunk tank's metal target.

Splash!

The platform suddenly dropped, and, for

the first time that day, Ben fell right into the soapy water!

Raven was horrified.

Ben swam to the side of the tank, and Raven said, "I am so sorry. That was a total accident."

"Why is this water all soapy?" asked Ben, spitting suds out of his mouth.

"The water's all soapy because I put soap in it," Raven confessed.

"Why would you do that?" asked Ben, confused.

"Because I'm a real jerk," she answered.

"No, no. You're not a jerk," said Ben right away. "You're my friend."

Raven took a deep breath. Real friends were honest with each other. Raven knew that.

Ben might get real angry with her. He might even quit their project—and then her grade would be trashed. But Raven couldn't lie anymore and pretend everything was okay when it wasn't.

"Okay," Raven told Ben, "so, as a friend, here goes. Ben . . . you stink. All right, I'm sorry."

"I do?" asked Ben.

He didn't look angry at all to Raven. Just confused. Raven didn't understand. Didn't Ben *know*?

"Ben, I mean, hasn't anybody ever told you that before?" Raven asked him.

"Well, my mom," said Ben. "But that's just my mom. She thinks my dad smells, too."

"Interesting," said Raven. Obviously, like father, like son applies here! she thought.

"Well, I guess I could just shower more," he said with a shrug. "It's no big deal."

"Great!" Raven's face brightened. She'd actually gotten through to him. Only now she felt a little guilty. She decided to take the edge off a little. "As long as that's what you want, Ben," she said, "because I . . . I mean, I don't care if you shower."

"Oh . . . then I won't," said Ben.

"All right," said Raven. But it wasn't the answer she was hoping for!

Well, no harm done, thought Raven. Maybe this boy just needs a little show-and-tell.

Grabbing a cleaning brush out of a nearby bucket, Raven took hold of Ben's head and began scrubbing behind his ear. Then she reached under his arm.

Rub-a-dub-dub! she sang to herself.

Ben started to laugh.

Okay, so he's ticklish, thought Raven. But I'm not stopping till this boy smells as fresh as a mountain spring!

As Ben climbed out of the soapy water, all squeaky-clean and mountain-spring fresh, he saw someone else was already replacing him on the dunk tank's platform.

Apparently, one of the carnival organizers had figured out *why* nobody was buying any food at the barbecue stand. So he gave Mr. Lawler a new job—one out of *spitting* range of the carnival refreshments.

As Ben toweled off his wet hair, he told his teacher about Raven and how cool she was for being so honest about the stinky thing.

"Son," said Mr. Lawler settling into his seat on the dunk tank platform, "when you have a p-problem, and p-people don't p-point it out, you lose p-perspective."

Ben was interested in what the teacher had to say, but no matter how much he dodged and weaved, he just couldn't avoid being hit by Lawler's spit storm!

"If I had a p-problem," continued Lawler, "I would not want p-people to beat around the bush-sh. Son, I have one word that will change your life. . . ."

Oh, man, thought Ben, whatever that word is, I hope there's not a P in it.

No such luck.

"That one word," said Lawler, "is antip-p-p-p-erspirant!"

The spit spray was so bad this time, Ben decided to make like Raven and press the dunk-tank lever—but this time on *purpose*.

"P-Pathetic!" cried Mr. Lawler before his body sent water flying in all directions.

Ben couldn't help smiling. His teacher may have sprayed him with one last *splash*, but it was Ben who'd gotten the last *laugh*!

Part Two

Chapter One

"So," said Raven, walking toward her next class at Bayside Junior High, "last night I was at Burger-rama, and the new guy was sitting a few tables away."

Raven's best friend, Chelsea Daniels, scratched her head. New guy? she wondered. "You mean the guy with the—"

"No," said Raven.

"Oh, the guy with the—"

"Yeah," said Raven.

"Love him," said Chelsea with a dreamy smile.

Just then, Raven's other best friend, Eddie Thomas, walked up to them. "Hi," he said.

"He's so cute!" Chelsea gushed.

Uh-oh, thought Eddie. If the girls were gushin', then he was rushin'. "Oh, bye," he said, dashing off.

He'd *almost* escaped, too. But Raven grabbed his shirt and yanked him back.

"So, anyway," Raven continued, "I looked at him, and then he looked away. And then he looked at me, and I looked away. And then we totally ignored each other . . . I mean, we *really* connected. Can you believe it, girl? I got a boyfriend!"

"Aaaaahh!" Raven and Chelsea shrieked with excitement.

Both of them looked at Eddie, waiting for *his* reaction.

"Ah!" he said with a halfhearted shrug.

"I can't wait to meet him, Rae!" Chelsea cried.

"Yeah, me, too," said Raven.

"What?" cried Eddie. He shook his head in

exasperation. Raven and Chelsea were flipping out over some guy Raven hadn't even *met* yet. Why were girls such . . . such . . . *psychos*? Eddie thought.

"Oh, there he is!" Raven cried. "Him."

Her "boyfriend" was really tall, which was why Raven had worn her new superstacked platforms today. She'd also clipped a bright red flower into her hair. The color matched her red turtleneck and super-diva faux-fur jacket, which she wore with a pair of distressed jeans.

I am lookin' so fine, it's almost a crime! she thought as she rushed up to the tall, handsome guy.

He was looking fine, too, in a pair of baggy cargo pants and a denim vest. The only issue Raven had was the shirt he wore under his vest—a ratty fleece number that did *nothing* for him. Note to self, thought Raven, ask my boyfriend to burn that shirt before we go out!

Eddie and Chelsea watched as Raven fell into step behind the guy. Then she motioned to her friends, pointing to the boy and then to herself, as if she were totally "with" him.

The guy never even noticed.

When Raven rejoined her friends, she said, "Don't we look fabulous together? Except for that shirt. That's got to go."

"Okay," said Eddie, "I think this really needs to be said. You don't *know* him!"

When they reached Eddie's locker, he was relieved. He turned away just as Amber walked up.

Amber was pretty and bubbly and one of the most popular girls in school. She always threw parties. And she *always* had a boyfriend.

"Hey, guys," Amber said, tossing her shoulder-length dark hair.

"What's up, Amber?" said Raven.

"Don't forget about my party this weekend.

I'll be there with my boyfriend, of course. And Ryan's taking Lisa," she said pointing to a girl down the hall. "And Ellie's going with Carter."

Then she looked Raven and Chelsea up and down. "And you two can go with . . . each other. But you know what? That's *okay*."

Raven could not believe the attitude on this girl. Time she heard the news! thought Raven.

"Excuse me, little Miss Missy, all right," said Raven, getting right in Amber's I'm-all-that face. "But I *have* a boyfriend."

"Oh, perfect," said Amber backing off.

After Amber left, Chelsea glared at Raven. It was one thing for just the two of them to play the "he's my boyfriend" game. But announcing it to Amber was a different story.

"What?" said Raven, looking at her friend's annoyed face.

Chelsea put her hands on her hips. "And

now for a reality update. That guy is *not* your boyfriend. And that's *okay*."

"You know what? He is," snapped Raven. "He's just in denial. Okay? Don't worry about it. We are going to get you a boyfriend because we are not going to that party without one. All right?"

As Eddie rejoined them, Raven suddenly froze—

Through her eye
The vision runs
Flash of future
Here it comes—

I see all three of us—me, Eddie, and Chelsea.

We're standing together in the school hall-way and—uh-oh, not good. We're screaming. We're screaming with dread!

Suddenly, the scene changes. I see a class-room. Mr. Lawler's classroom. Oh, no. Not "spit storm" Lawler!

There's a desk chair in the front row. It's the very seat Mr. Lawler stands in front of as he teaches class—

And it's the only seat left empty!

Raven's vision ended abruptly. When she shook her head clear, she found Chelsea star-ing at her.

"Rae, what'd you see?" she asked.

"I saw Lawler's class," Raven told her. "And one of us is getting *the seat*!"

"Aaaaahh!" Chelsea and Eddie shrieked.

Raven held her ears. Everyone at Bayside knew the horrors of getting "the seat" in Lawler's class. But she really didn't want to lose her *hearing* over it!

"Yeah, I know," Raven told her friends,

"but I don't know which one of us it was."

"Wait a minute," said Eddie. "We don't even *have* Lawler's class."

Just then, Raven overheard Amber telling one of her friends, "Lawler's taking over first period. And he's starting a whole new seating chart!"

"I cannot get that seat! No way!" cried Chelsea.

"Wait, wait, wait," Eddie told her. "Let's just calm down, take a breath and approach this rationally—"

Raven thought that made sense. She took a deep breath, and was just finding her calm and peaceful "center" when Eddie lost it. He grabbed her by the shoulders and shook her senseless.

"Is it me?" he shrieked. "Think, woman, think!"

Just then, the bell rang.

"I know that stare," Raven said.
"That's the 'Crystal' stare."

"Ben Sturky!" Raven cried in disgust,
pinching her nose.

"I finally figured out what was
so gross about me in your vision,"
Eddie told Raven.

"There's no way I'm going to the carnival
tomorrow," Eddie said. "I'm calling Crystal
and saying I'm sick."

"I can't move my face," Eddie said.

"Have no fear, family!" Cory announced.
"I'm going to *blow* the stink away."

"It's so great that you volunteered
to help out with the dunk tank,"
Raven said to Ben Sturky.

"So, what do you *really* look like?"
Eddie asked Raven.

"Don't worry about it," Raven said. "We are going to get you a boyfriend because we are not going to that party without one."

"I saw Lawler's class," Raven said. "And one of us is getting *the seat*!"

"See?" said Chelsea. "Totally not clingy."

"Who cares if he has the same name as your dog?" Raven said to Chelsea.

"Nickname! That's what we can do!"
Raven cried. "We can give him
a nickname."

"We are going to Amber's party—*together*,"
Raven told Chelsea.

**I am ready and set, so bring on the wet!
Eddie thought.**

**"No one messes with my girl,"
Raven said.**

Eddie, Raven, and Chelsea all screamed.

Like a shot, Eddie took off down the hall. Chelsea followed. But where was Raven?

Chelsea turned to find her best friend inching down the hallway with baby steps.

"First come, first served. Raven, run!" cried Chelsea.

Raven was practically in tears. She pointed to her new superstacked platforms. "Girl, in these shoes, this *is* running!"

Chapter Two

Eddie was the first of the three friends to arrive in Mr. Lawler's classroom. Almost every seat was taken. "The seat" was still empty, of course—front row, center.

Frantically, Eddie searched the room. There had to be at least one more empty seat left. There *had* to be!

And there was! In fact, there were *two*! Eddie headed for the back row to nab one, when a girl stood up and blocked him.

Then she placed little handwritten "reserved" signs on the desktops.

Eddie was about to argue with the girl, when he heard his best friend's voice.

"Reservations for Raven?"

Raven strode up with Chelsea and each of the girls took one of the reserved seats.

Eddie just stood there, his mouth open. How did Raven *do* that? Was it some sort of psychic trick?

Raven shot a "sorry" glance at her friend and revealed the secret weapon in her hand. "You really need to get a cell phone. All right?"

Eddie couldn't believe it. Raven had actually called ahead to get reservations—for English class!

"Mr. Thomas, have a seat," called Mr. Lawler from the front of the room.

Dragging himself slowly to "the seat," Eddie finally sat down at the dreaded desk. The spit storm began, almost immediately.

"P-People. P-People, p-please!" cried Mr. Lawler, spittle spewing from his mouth like Yellowstone's Old Faithful. "Settle, p-please . . . Tyrell . . . P-Patty . . . P-Please!"

Eddie flinched as every sputtering "P" spritzed him with a new spray of Mr. Lawler's saliva.

"P-Pay attention, p-people!"

Eddie sighed and wiped his face. He could see this was going to be the longest—and wettest—period of his school day.

As the class dragged on, Eddie tried to visualize pleasant things: surfing on the ocean, white-water rafting, Hawaiian waterfalls.

But Lawler's voice just kept droning on— "That is why p-punctuality is a p-pet p-peeve of mine. I cannot say it enough. P-Punctuality, p-punctuality, p-punctuality!"

Oh, please, thought Eddie. For my sake, *stop* saying it! Then he wiped more spit from his cheek.

Raven felt bad for Eddie. But she sure was glad it was him and not her!

Suddenly, Lawler's voice faded away, and the whole room froze—

Through her eye
The vision runs
Flash of future
Here it comes—

I see Chelsea.

She's standing by our lockers, holding some books, and talking to a dark-haired boy in a beige jacket.

I can't see the boy's face—just the back of his head and shoulders. But I can see Chelsea's face. Her smile is flashing brighter than the sun's glare, and her eyes are all wide like she's totally blissed-out.

Now she's starting to laugh, and—ohmigosh! She's snorting. Chelsea's actually snorting!

You go, girlfriend! You're in love!

Raven was so wrapped up in her vision of Chelsea meeting a boy, she didn't even hear Mr. Lawler speaking to her.

Mr. Lawler was saying. "Raven B-Baxter. Miss B-Baxter. Miss B-Baxter!"

With every "B," a new spray of spit soaked Eddie. Finally, he couldn't take it anymore. Turning in his seat, he yelled, "*Answer* him!"

Shaking her head clear, Raven looked at Eddie who begged her, "*Please* don't make him say your name again!"

"Oh! I'm so sorry," said Raven. "That was so rude, Mr. Lawler. And may I say that science would have to be my favorite subject."

"Excellent. Too bad this is *English*," said the teacher. "Which is why you'll each be getting a copy of *Oliver T-twist*, the t-tragic t-tale of a t-tortured youth-th."

"I can relate," muttered Eddie, as he swiped the spit off his desk and onto the floor.

"Miss B-Baxter," said Mr. Lawler, "p-please p-pass out the reading lists."

Mr. Lawler handed Raven a pile of papers, and she rose to pass them out.

When she reached Chelsea, she whispered, "Girl, you are not gonna believe this!"

Chelsea's eyes widened.

"I just saw you with a—guyyyy!" Raven cried.

Just then, one of Raven's superstacked platforms slipped on the puddle of spit Eddie had made when he'd wiped off his desk.

That's all right, thought Raven, on her way down. I may hit the floor, but Chelsea will get her boy. Double-dating, here I come!

Chapter Three

"So, cool," Raven told Chelsea after class. "I found my boyfriend at Burger-rama and you are gonna find yours somewhere in all this—" Raven gestured to the crowd in the hallway.

"Raven, once again, you are making way too big a deal out of this," said Chelsea. "All you saw in your vision was me talking to some guy."

"A really cute guy," Raven pointed out.

"But you only saw the back of his head," said Chelsea.

"A really cute back of his head," Raven assured her.

"How do you know I even *liked* him?" asked Chelsea.

"Because you did your . . ." Raven imitated Chelsea's little laugh and snort.

"I *snorted*?" asked Chelsea, suddenly intrigued.

"Big-time," said Raven.

Chelsea hated to admit it, but if Raven saw her *snorting* over this guy, maybe he really was worth finding.

"We've got to find this guy," said Chelsea, pulling Raven down the hall.

Raven hadn't seen the guy's face in her vision. But she'd seen the back of his head. That was *something* to go on, at least. So she started checking out the backs of guys' heads as they walked toward their lockers.

It didn't take long for Chelsea to become really frustrated.

"Rae, this is crazy," she said. "What do I care about bringing a guy to Amber's stupid party?"

"Uh, Chels, this is bigger than a party. All right, this is the year we're gonna have boyfriends *together*. I found mine, and now you're gonna find yours—" Raven stopped when she saw Chelsea scribbling madly in her notebook.

"Okay, what are you writing?" asked Raven.

Chelsea ripped out the page and held it up. The word BOY was written in big bold letters—and then crossed out.

"You don't have a boyfriend, okay?" said Chelsea. "Read it. Memorize it. Eat it." She threw the paper at Raven and strode over to her locker.

"You're missing the point," said Raven, trying not to lose her patience. "We could double-date. I am talking parties together . . . movies . . . dancing."

Chelsea reached into her locker and pulled out a bag of chips. "Do you mind if I eat while you nag?"

"Fine," Raven replied huffily. "But don't

blame me when you're all alone at Amber's party, stuffing your face full of chips, while I'm with my boyfriend, and all you can say is—"

Raven reached into the bag, grabbed a chip, shoved it into her mouth, and garbled, "I wish I'd listened to Raven."

"Look, Rae, I know you mean well, but I'll meet him when I meet him, okay?"

Chelsea slammed her locker shut, turned to go, and—*Bam!* She walked right into a boy.

"I am *so* sorry," said Chelsea, as books and papers flew everywhere.

"Oh, it's okay," the boy replied.

Both of them started picking up their things. And in the middle of the mess, they locked eyes.

"Hi," said the boy.

"Hi," said Chelsea.

Wow, this guy is really hot, thought Chelsea. He was tall with dark hair and big beautiful puppy-dog eyes. And the way those eyes were looking at Chelsea, she got the feeling he thought *she* was hot, too!

Without thinking, Chelsea gave a nervous little laugh—and snorted.

Ohmigosh, thought Raven, watching the whole thing. Chelsea snorted! Chelsea snorted!

Instantly, Raven yanked her best friend away. "That's *him*. That's the guy. You even did the laugh!"

"Did I snort?" asked Chelsea.

"Like a pig," said Raven.

"Aaaaahh!" they screamed excitedly.

"Okay, okay, calm, calm," said Raven. "What's his name?"

"Well, you pulled me away before I could ask," said Chelsea.

"No, Chels, I pulled you away before you looked like this—" Raven twisted her features into a totally blissed-out, dumbstruck face.

Chelsea giggled.

Just then, Eddie walked over to them. He'd survived the first day sitting in Mr. Lawler's dreaded front-row seat. But he didn't look too happy about it.

A couple of boys walked by laughing and pointing at Eddie's wet shirt. "What's up, Splash Mountain?" one of them yelled, then cracked up again.

Eddie sighed, turned to Raven and Chelsea, and asked, "You know what's worse than warm spit?"

They shook their heads.

"*Cold* spit," he told them, pulling at his saliva-streaked shirt.

"Hey, Eddie, you know those shirts in the Lost and Found that are better off lost?" asked Raven. "Go find one."

As Eddie did, Chelsea tugged on the sleeve of Raven's faux-fur jacket. She pointed down the hall. That hot-looking boy had turned around.

"Rae, he's coming over," Chelsea whispered in a panic. "What do I do?"

"Just be yourself," said Raven. "Play hard to get. Don't be all clingy."

"I am *not* clingy," she protested. But when Raven shrugged and turned away, Chelsea lunged for her friend. "Wait! Don't leave me!"

"Girl, please," said Raven, detaching Chelsea from her arm.

As Raven disappeared around the corner, Chelsea pulled herself together. She was actually pretty calm by the time Mr. Wonderful walked up to her and said, "I grabbed your history book by mistake."

"Oh, thanks," said Chelsea, as they exchanged books.

"Look, I have history next, too. You walking over?" he asked.

Chelsea was about to answer when she heard the kid behind her slam his locker shut. *Uh-oh.*

"Um, not right away," Chelsea told the guy calmly.

"Well, maybe I'll see you at lunch," he said.

"Yeah, that'd be great," she replied.

The second Mr. Wonderful left, Raven ran over. "Heard it all," she said. "Love that you didn't go with him."

"Yeah," said Chelsea, "I just let him walk right on by. Didn't even budge an inch."

"And totally not clingy," Raven said, super-impressed with her girl. Chelsea had played it really cool, thought Raven. Yeah, Chels had come a long way!

The bell rang, and the hall cleared out.

Only Chelsea was left, standing by the lockers. She wanted to go to class—she really did. But she couldn't—because she was *stuck.*

When that kid behind Chelsea had slammed his locker shut earlier, he'd caught the hood of Chelsea's sweater inside the door!

That was the *real* reason Chelsea hadn't gone off with Mr. Wonderful. She couldn't move! She was just glad Raven hadn't figured it out.

Now, Chelsea just had to free herself and get to class!

"Oh, oh, man," grumbled Chelsea, twisting and turning as she pulled at her caught sweater. "Oh, come on!"

Just then, Raven peeked back around the corner to find Chelsea playing tug-of-war with a school locker.

"See?" said Chelsea, struggling with her sweater. "Totally not clingy."

Raven just shook her head. What was she going to do with this girl?

Chapter Four

By the time lunch period came around, Eddie had found some dry clothes. He grabbed a table in the corner—far, far away from today's faculty monitor.

In the middle of the room, Mr. Lawler was already gushing like a fountain.

"P-Pep-peroni p-pizza!" the teacher said as he spied a girl's lunch tray.

She covered the food with her hands, but it was already too late. Lawler's spit spray had done its damage.

"P-Pipe down, P-Paul, and eat your p-pudding," Mr. Lawler told another student.

Needless to say, the boy's spit-sprayed pudding was going into the garbage!

Eddie laughed to himself. Too bad for those kids, he thought. But at least I'll be staying dry *this* period, along with my lunch.

Raven walked over to Eddie's table and sat down. She stared at his sweater. It was pink. And it had a big red heart across the chest.

Oh, that's right, Raven thought to herself. It wasn't *his* sweater. It was the sweater he'd picked up from the school's Lost and Found bin.

"I like that," Raven told him. "I *have* that."

"It was either this or a tube top," said Eddie flatly.

Meanwhile, over at the next table, Chelsea was eating lunch with that cute boy she'd met earlier.

"Well," he was telling her, "I sort of like history."

"I like it, too," said Chelsea right away. "I mean, I guess it's because I'm really good at dates." Chelsea froze when she realized how that sounded. "In *history*," she quickly added. "*Dates* in history!"

Mr. Wonderful smiled. "So, what are you doing after school?" he asked.

Oh, wow, thought Chelsea dreamily. Looks like that "dates" mistake was a good idea, after all!

"Um, nothing—" she started to tell him. But she stopped when she noticed Raven frantically waving a piece of yellow notebook paper at the next table. Chelsea read the paper. CLINGY was written on it.

Raven's right, thought Chelsea, I don't want to look clingy . . . I better fix this.

"Um, nothing—*that I could just possibly get out of,*" she finally told Mr. Wonderful. "Busy, busy, busy me!"

"Well, how 'bout tomorrow after school?" asked the boy.

"Yeah. Sure," said Chelsea.

At the next table, Raven smiled. She was glad to see her girl was doing so well. But, suddenly, Raven felt the world freeze around her—

Through her eye
The vision runs
Flash of future
Here it comes—

I see Chelsea.

She's in her bedroom, sitting on the carpet.

"I can't get rid of Sam. No way," she calls toward her speakerphone.

Now she's getting up off the floor and walking over to her bed. Her big basset hound, Sam, is lying there, blinking his sweet brown eyes.

"Because he's my Sammy," says Chelsea, scratching her dog's long floppy ears. "Yes,

you are. Yes, you are. My little Sammy Wammy boy!"

When Raven came out of her vision, she loudly whispered, "Chelsea!"

But Chelsea didn't notice.

"*Psst*, Chelsea!" Raven repeated.

But Chelsea *still* didn't notice.

Eddie sighed. This could go on for the entire lunch period! Frustrated, he picked up the doughnut on his tray and threw it at Chelsea's table. Unfortunately, it ended up bouncing off her forehead. Oh, well, thought Eddie, at least it got her attention!

As Chelsea looked up, Eddie explained, "Raven wants you."

Chelsea smiled politely at her guy. "This will just take a second," she told him. "Sorry."

She stormed over to Raven's table and plopped down. "What?" she snapped.

"I just had a vision that someone wants you to get rid of your dog," said Raven, upset. She began taking big nervous gulps from her bottle of spring water.

"No way." Chelsea couldn't believe it. She loved her dog! She'd never get rid of him! That vision was just wrong. "Like I'd ever give up my little Sam."

"Yeah?" called Chelsea's Mr. Wonderful from the next table.

Chelsea turned around. "Excuse me?"

"Well, you said my name," the boy explained. "Sam."

Mr. Wonderful had the same name as Chelsea's dog! Raven spit an entire mouthful of water all over Eddie's dry sweater.

Whoops, thought Raven, looks like Eddie is going to be wearing that Lost and Found tube top for the rest of the school day.

"Your name's Sam?" Chelsea asked the cute

boy. She couldn't believe it. Shocked, she turned to Raven and whispered, "He's another little Sammy Wammy boy!"

Raven and Eddie had to bite their tongues to keep from laughing.

Unfortunately, Mr. Wonderful didn't see what was so funny. "I'm a *what*?" he asked.

Raven ran over to Sam's table, determined to fix this situation right up.

"Sam," said Raven, "she calls all her guys that." Thinking fast, she pointed to Eddie. "That's her little 'Eddie Weddie boy.'"

Eddie had been busy drying himself off. But when he heard *that*, he looked up. "Okay, you call me that?" he asked Chelsea. "That's *gotta* stop."

"And we gotta go," said Raven.

Raven started to drag Chelsea away.

"I'll walk you out," said Sam, rising from his seat.

"No, Sam! Stay!" commanded Chelsea.

Sam stayed.

"Sam, sit," said Raven.

Sam sat.

"Good boy," said Eddie, trying not to crack up.

"You guys," said Chelsea as the three of them huddled near the lunchroom door, "I'm supposed to meet him after school tomorrow. What am I going to do? Every time I say his name now, I'm going to think of my dog!"

"Look," said Raven, "who cares if he has the same name as your dog? He is so fine."

"Yeah, he is cute isn't he?" Chelsea said dreamily. "This is so silly." She turned back to Mr. Wonderful. "Hey, Sam!" she called.

But when he turned around and smiled, all Chelsea could see was her dog's panting face. She burst out laughing. She just couldn't help it!

From her point of view, Mr. Wonderful had suddenly grown the long nose and floppy ears of her basset hound—and his big puppy-dog eyes now looked like *real* puppy-dog eyes!

When Sam stared at her as if she'd lost her marbles, Chelsea panicked. She quickly turned and ran out of the lunchroom.

"Don't worry," Raven told Sam before racing after her friend, "she likes you, you lucky dog!"

Chapter Five

That night, Raven and Chelsea were talking on their speakerphones.

"I still can't believe I met a guy named Sam," said Chelsea, finishing her nightly sit-ups on her bedroom floor.

Hearing his name, Chelsea's dog sat up on her bed and barked.

"You know what," said Raven. "The party is this Saturday. Just get over it and ask him to go."

"Sure—as soon as you ask *your* boyfriend," said Chelsea. "You know, you would say, 'Hey, do you wanna go to the party Saturday?' And then he'd say, 'And you are . . . ?'"

"Okay, listen, Little Miss Missy," snapped Raven, sitting higher in her seat at the kitchen counter. "All right, I *spoke* to my boyfriend. We had a little conversation."

"Get out," said Chelsea, surprised. "You did? What'd he say?"

"Let me tell you," said Raven. "Okay, I called him, right? And he said, 'Hello.' And then I said, 'Is this Ernie's Pizza?' And then—in the *cutest* way—he said, 'No.' And then he hung up. Girl, it was magical."

Raven's father, who'd been busy cooking nearby, suddenly added, "And then her father said, in the *cutest* way, 'Get off the phone!' And she did. And it was so *magical*!"

"Dad, this is serious, all right?" said Raven, annoyed by his lame attempt at humor. "This is about Amber's party."

"Amber's having a party and she didn't invite me?" said Mr. Baxter in a high-pitched voice. "That is *so* like her."

Raven rolled her eyes, and her father spoke

up again. But this time, her dad wasn't trying to be funny.

"Chelsea, look," he said into the speakerphone. "Why don't you just change your dog's name?"

"But that's his name," said Chelsea. "I can't get rid of Sam. No way."

Chelsea crossed her bedroom and began to hug the big basset hound on her bed. "Because he's my Sammy," she began to coo in baby talk, just like Raven's vision. "Yes, you are. Yes, you are. My little Sammy Wammy boy!"

On the other end of the line, Raven was about to answer Chelsea, when her little brother Cory interrupted.

"Homework," he said, pointing to the laptop in front of Raven. "I need the computer."

"Get away, maggot," said Raven.

"Okay, fine," said Cory, all indignant. "Undermine my education. Step on the hopes and dreams our father has for his children."

"Boy," said Mr. Baxter, "I'd be happy if you just *flushed.*"

Raven shook her head and handed over the laptop to Cory.

"Rae," said Chelsea over the speakerphone, "it's not that I don't want a boyfriend. It's just maybe this guy's not the one."

When Raven's little brother heard Chelsea's voice, he immediately picked up the receiver. "And I agree. Chelsea, Cory here. Listen, I heard about your problem, and if you need someone to talk to . . . or *watch you exercise,* I'm here for you, baby."

Chelsea shook her head. "You still wear the pajamas, you know, the ones with the bunny feet . . . *baby?*"

"Well, baby—" Cory started.

"Hand over the phone, worm," Raven interrupted.

Cory did. But first he gave the receiver a little wipe down—with his tongue.

"Eww!" cried Raven. She glared at her father.

"Don't look at me," said Mr. Baxter. "The boy is good."

"And my nickname isn't 'worm' or 'maggot,'" he informed his sister. "It's Doctor Love."

Most of the time, Raven had no use for her little brother. But this time, she had to admit, he'd given her a great idea.

"Nickname, girl, nickname! That's what we can do," she cried, quickly putting the phone back up to her ear. "We can give him a nickname. Then you can call him anything you want."

Oh, man, thought Raven. This receiver is *soaking wet*!

"And for your FYI," she told Chelsea, "I have Cory's spit in my ear. *Eww!* Call you later."

"It's not gonna work, honey," said Mr. Baxter as Raven hung up. "There's only one place where guys can get a good nickname. Unfortunately, girls aren't allowed."

"Where?" asked Raven.

"Aha. Tell her, son," said Mr. Baxter.

Cory struck a muscleman pose. "The gym!" he shouted.

Raven frowned.

Her nickname idea was too good to give up on. She'd just have to find some way to make it work.

Chapter Six

The next day, during gym class, Eddie emerged from the boys' locker room and stood just outside the double doors that led into the gym.

Just behind him stood Raven and Chelsea. Before meeting up with Eddie, the two had changed in the girls' locker room—just as they'd planned. Mission "Rename Chelsea's Boyfriend" was about to begin!

Raven and Chelsea nodded their "okay," and Eddie poked his head through the gym doors. He saw a group of guys working out their moves on the basketball court. Chelsea's Mr. Wonderful was one of them.

Sam dribbled the ball across the floor and

eased it right into the basket. Not bad, thought Eddie, looks like Chelsea's boyfriend is a pretty good player.

"Nice shot!" somebody cried.

Eddie pushed through the doors and strutted into the gym. He took a few steps toward the court, then glanced behind him—but nobody was there.

Where the heck are they? he wondered.

"Get out here!" he called over his shoulder.

Raven slowly peeked through the double doors. Gathering her courage, she finally pushed through and swaggered in, trying to walk like Eddie.

She'd dressed like him, too, and all the other boys in class. She was wearing yellow sweats with BAYSIDE BARRACUDAS written across the shirt. Unlike the other boys, however, she'd stuffed her long hair beneath a backward baseball cap. And she'd worn sunglasses, just to make sure none of the guys recognized her.

Chelsea was wearing a baseball cap and sunglasses just like Raven. But when Raven turned around, her best girlfriend was nowhere in sight!

"Chelsea! Get out here," Raven called to the gym doors.

Chelsea finally came through, too, trying to swagger like one of the boys. But she failed miserably.

"Are your drawers riding up or something?" asked Raven. Chelsea stopped in her tracks.

"No. Like this," Raven told her. She took a few steps forward, rolling her shoulders as she walked.

Chelsea did her best to copy Raven's walk. Eddie joined in. The three of them strutted across the hardwood floor.

"Yeah," Eddie said. "It's all about the shoulders. It's *all* about the shoulders. Yeah, yeah."

Eddie turned and studied the girls' moves. He nodded approvingly. "You got it! Yeah. All right!"

Then Raven spotted that new boy—the tall, handsome one who had ignored her in Burger-rama. The one who had said "no" when she'd called his house and asked if it was Ernie's Pizza.

"There's my boyfriend!" she cried, and totally forgot about the whole make-like-a-boy thing.

Going completely girly, Raven winked and smiled as he swaggered by.

Eddie grabbed her and pulled her back. "No! No! Raven, no, no, no."

But Raven wasn't listening. "We're gonna make such a cute couple when I'm a girl again." She sighed, blowing him a kiss.

"Let's just get in the game," Eddie told Raven. As he went, he gave Chelsea a manly slap on the shoulder. But the blow knocked Chelsea's shoulder pads out of place. She and Raven scrambled to fix them.

From the sidelines, the girls watched as Sam guarded the basket. A player shot, but Sam blocked his move. Then the coach blew the whistle.

"Moving pick!" the coach yelled. "No moving your feet when you block! You *know* that, Sam."

Raven heard the coach.

"Pick," she said, trying to make a nickname out of it. "Pick, picker, nose picker, booger, booger . . . Booger!"

Settling on her choice, Raven turned and cheered for Sam. "Way to go, Booger! All right, Booger, Booger . . ."

Chelsea hit Raven's shoulder. That nickname was awful! "Chelsea and Booger?" she cried, disgusted.

"Oh, sure!" Raven replied. "If you say it like *that*!"

As Chelsea and Raven watched the game, Sam got control of the ball. He dribbled across the court and jumped high enough to jam the ball through the hoop.

"Okay, okay, that's what I want to see," the coach cried. "Nice dunk! Nice dunk, Sam."

Raven blinked in thought and ran through these new options. "Dunk. Dunker. Dunkey!"

Then she ran up to Sam and began to cheer. "Way to go, Dunkey! Whoo, whoo, whoo . . . all right!"

Under her sunglasses, Chelsea rolled her eyes. "Great! I've gone from a dog to a *donkey*."

"No," said Raven, "but if you say *dunk*—"

"No!" Chelsea cried, cutting her off. "That's what I'm trying to tell you—"

As they argued, the coach blew his whistle into their ears. Raven and Chelsea both jumped.

"I don't know you, do I?" demanded the coach, hands on hips. "But I *do* know that those sunglasses are against the rules."

The girls quickly pulled off their sunglasses.

"It's a silly rule," the coach told them. "But you know who made it up?"

Raven and Chelsea shook their heads.

"Me!" shouted the coach. "Now, names!"

"Uh, I'm Bill," said Raven in a deep voice.

"And I'm Bob," said Chelsea in an even deeper voice.

"Last names!" barked the coach.

Chelsea looked at Raven—who couldn't think of a thing.

"Uh . . . Bob!" Chelsea cried, thinking fast.

"Bob Bob?" said the coach, scratching his head.

Raven nodded. "Yeah, Coach," she said. "And I'm *Bill* Bob."

"We, uh, we're cousins. Right, Bob?" said Chelsea.

"Bill," Raven corrected her.

Chelsea laughed nervously. "See? Even *we* get confused."

The coach frowned. "Well, let me see if I can *un*confuse you."

He pointed to Chelsea. "You're shirts." Then, to Raven, "and you're skins."

The coach clapped his hands and pointed. "Shirts over there. Skins over there. Move!"

"All right!" Chelsea cried. "All right. Shirts!"

"I'm a skin! I'm a skin, all right," chanted Raven. But when she joined the rest of her teammates, Raven paused and asked them, "Yo, what's a skin?"

The coach blew his whistle. All the guys around Raven pulled off their sweatshirts.

"Oh, snap," said Raven. She crossed the gym to join Chelsea, chanting, "I'm a shirt, I'm a shirt, I'm a shirt, shirt, shirt."

Raven sidled up to Chelsea. "Whoo, we're shirts!" She poked Chelsea in the ribs. "Girl, we *gotta* get outta here!"

Chelsea frowned. "But they're going to let me play guard."

Just then, Raven noticed Eddie was being hassled by some of the guys at the other end of the court.

"How's the seat, DJ Dribble?" said one guy.

"Yeah, spit for brains," said another.

They all laughed. Then they all started rappin'.

"Sittin' in the seat, soaked to his feet."

"Everybody knows that the fool is dead meat. . . ."

"We ain't jokin', this kid is soakin'. . . . No we ain't jokin', this kid is soakin'."

After they finished, they all laughed and high-fived each other.

Eddie shook his head. "You know what?" he said. "Let *me* break it down for you."

Then Eddie began *his* rap.

"I may be sittin' in the seat, soaked to my feet, but this homeboy has got you beat . . . You can call me names, makin' funny faces by the dozen. But you're nothing but a bunch of sad-rappin' cousins.

"You think you're so smart, you get F's and D's and *your* grades are so low, man, you get straight Z's. . . . I may be stuck sittin' through spit and spray, but it doesn't really matter cause I'm a'get an *A*!"

The other guys shook their heads. Eddie had won that rappin' round, and they knew it.

"Way to go, Eddie!" Raven cried.

As the group of guys walked off, Raven and Chelsea gave their boy high fives.

"Man," said Chelsea, impressed. "You're getting an *A* in Lawler's class?"

Eddie shrugged. "I don't know, but it rhymes."

Then Chelsea headed for the door.

"Hey, where are you going?" Raven asked.

"I got a boyfriend to meet," Chelsea replied. "If Eddie can get over being stuck with the seat, I can get over a stupid name."

Raven grinned. "That's my girl! We are *so* double-dating this weekend."

Chelsea breezed through the gym doors. Raven started to follow. Then, suddenly, she froze in her tracks—

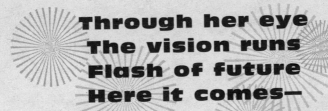

**Through her eye
The vision runs
Flash of future
Here it comes—**

I see the boys' locker room.

Whoa. Do I want to see the boys' locker room? Oh-no! But I have to . . . 'cause Sam's here. This vision's about Chelsea's boyfriend!

Sam is talking with a couple of boys in his gym class. They're all wearing white towels wrapped around their waists—well, thank goodness for that!

"Hey, you guys," Sam says, "wanna shoot some hoops after school?"

One of the guys frowns. "I thought you were meeting that girl after school."

Sam shakes his head. "Chelsea? Nah. It's just not there for me."

When Raven came out of her vision, Eddie was staring at her.

"Rae," he said, "I don't like that face."

Raven sighed. "Yeah, well, I didn't like my vision."

Chapter Seven

In front of the girls' room mirror, Chelsea had transformed herself.

The sweats were gone, and so was the base-ball cap. She'd changed into jeans and a cool tie-dyed shirt, and she'd put on her makeup with care.

She was just brushing out her hair when Raven slipped through the door.

"Oh, good, you're here," said Chelsea, seeing her best friend. Then she struck a pose. "Okay, I'm meeting Sam. What do you think?"

Raven nodded. "You look good. You look *really* good," she said. "But, you know, I was thinking that dating a guy with the same name as your dog . . . you know . . . is really kind of bizarre."

Chelsea stared at her friend. "And dating a guy you don't really know is kinda . . . you know . . . bizarre-*er*!"

Raven shrugged. "I was just thinking he is not your type."

Chelsea blinked in amazement. "You mean, tall and really cute?"

"Yo, girl, that is *so* last year," Raven said. "Do you know what is in right now? The little, cute, short, dumpy guys. They are *so* cute!"

Just then, the girls' room door opened. Eddie slowly backed through it. In his face was Mr. Lawler.

"Your p-participation has p-positively improved, Mr. Thomas," said the teacher, spraying Eddie with spit, as usual. "Thanks to my new seating p-plan."

Eddie blinked against the drizzle. "Thanks,

Mr. Lawler. But, uh, nature calls." He closed the bathroom door behind him. Then Eddie noticed the girls.

"What are you two doing in the boys' bathroom?" he asked, outraged.

Raven and Chelsea said nothing. They just waited for Eddie to look around and realize they weren't in the boys' room. *He* was in the *girls'* room!

"Oh, okay," Eddie said with a groan. "This is bad. I'm outta here."

"Me, too," said Chelsea, gathering up her stuff. "I don't want to be late meeting Sam."

But as she headed for the door, Raven stopped her. "He's not gonna be there," she said.

"What?" said Chelsea.

"She saw it in a vision," Eddie explained.

Chelsea turned to face Raven.

"He said 'it' just wasn't there for him," Raven said sadly.

Chelsea bit her lip. "Oh," she whispered, clearly hurt.

"But look," said Raven, trying to sound upbeat. "What does *he* know, girl? He is crazy. Because you got it. All over you. You've got it!"

"Yeah," said Eddie, "you absolutely have 'it.' Maybe not my 'it,' you know, because we're friends, and friends don't look at friends' 'its.' But for lots of other guys, you definitely have 'it' goin' on!"

Chelsea sighed and shook her head. "Nice try, but bottom line is, I still don't have a boyfriend."

Raven took her friend's hands in hers. "Chelsea," she began. "Did we have a good year last year?"

"Yeah."

"And did we have boyfriends?" Raven asked.

"No," Chelsea replied. "But what about all that stuff you said about boyfriends and double dating?"

Raven sighed. "I said a lot of stuff. I was

wrong, all right? Sure it would be fun to date someone, but we don't have to date someone to have fun."

Raven looped her arm through Chelsea's.

"We are going to Amber's party—*together*," Raven declared. "And if we find boyfriends, it'll be because they are nice, sweet guys . . . who have *cars*."

Behind them, Eddie spoke up.

"Man!" he cried, reading the graffiti scrawled on one of the stall doors. "This Cheryl is *bad*. Is this her current number?"

The next day, Eddie was totally ready for Mr. Lawler's English class.

He'd cut two armholes and one head hole out of a green garbage bag. Then he pulled it over his head and down over his clothing like military rain gear. He'd even borrowed a friend's motorcycle helmet.

The kids in class applauded as Eddie took his seat and slapped down the helmet's plastic visor.

I am ready and set, so bring on the wet! Eddie thought.

Raven came to class in costume, too. She'd worn her "boy" disguise—yellow sweats, a backward baseball cap, and sunglasses.

She swaggered in, right up to Chelsea's Mr. Not-So-Wonderful, who was sitting at his desk.

"What up, dog?" Raven said in a deep "boy" voice.

Sam looked up, startled.

"I, uh, kinda like that girl you blew off," Raven told him. "Hope it's cool."

Sam shrugged. "Uh, yeah, no problem. Go for it."

"Good, 'cause she invited me to a Warriors/Laker game tonight. Floor seats."

"Oh, man!" Sam put his head down and beat it against his desk.

"Aw, yeah," said Raven, biting her tongue to keep from laughing. "Well, uh, peace out."

As Raven walked away, she stopped by Chelsea, who had been watching the whole thing with satisfaction.

"Rae, you were brilliant," she whispered.

"Yeah, well," said Raven, "no one messes with my girl."

As Raven left, she noticed Mr. Lawler, standing just outside the classroom door.

"You're doing a great job," she said, then gathered up a mouthful of saliva and added, "P-Perfect!"

Raven just couldn't resist spraying Mr. Lawler on the last word. That one was for Eddie!

Gaze into the future and take a sneak peek at the next *That's So Raven* story. . . .

Adapted by Alice Alfonsi
Based on the series created by
Michael Poryes
Susan Sherman
Based on the teleplay written
by Dava Savel

School was over and the stampede was on. Crowds of kids poured out the front doors of Bayside Junior High, making their break for freedom. Raven Baxter couldn't wait to join them.

"Oh, hey, Rae!" called Raven's best friend Chelsea Daniels from across the hall. "You want to come over and do that biology homework and rewrite that history paper?"

Homework? thought Raven, slamming her locker door shut. My girl needs a reality check. When school is done, you got to bring on the *fun*!

"I'm sorry," said Raven. "I didn't quite catch that."

Chelsea got the message. "You want to go shopping and get a pedicure?"

Raven grinned. "That's what I *thought* you said."

Suddenly, Raven froze. Every molecule of her body seemed to tingle, and time seemed to stop.

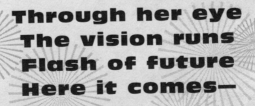

Through her eye
The vision runs
Flash of future
Here it comes—

I see my parents standing by the front door of my house, and—uh-oh, not good— they don't look happy.

Now they're opening their mouths. They're about to say something—

"No, no, and no!"

The vision ended as abruptly as it began. Raven blinked and said, "That was weird. I just had a vision of my parents saying 'no.'"

"About what?" asked Chelsea.

"Hello? They're parents," said Raven. "Do they *need* a reason?"

Just then, Raven noticed a good-looking older boy striding down the hallway. At the end of the corridor, he stopped and began to look around.

"Chelsea," she whispered, "look, there's that cute guy from the video store."

Chelsea checked him out. He had broad

shoulders and was holding a set of car keys. "Wait, he's in high school," she whispered to Raven. "What's he doing here?"

"I don't know, but teeth check!" cried Raven.

The "teeth check" was a move the girls had come up with back in grade school—the day after Raven had delivered a book report to her entire class with a piece of spinach stuck between her two front teeth.

Both Raven and Chelsea bared their teeth, and gave each other the once-over.

"You're good," the two said together.

Now for phase two of our "meet the cute guy" routine, thought Raven.

"Ha-ha-ha!" laughed Chelsea.

"Ha-ha-ha!" Raven laughed back.

They glanced in the cute boy's direction. He hadn't noticed them. Dang, thought Raven. She shot a look at Chelsea, and the two girls moved closer to him.

"Ha-ha-HA-HA!" laughed Chelsea, even louder.

"Ha-ha-HA-HA!" echoed Raven, louder still.

Okay, thought Raven, do *not* tell me you can't hear me *now*!

"Hey, Raven!" called the boy when he finally glanced over.

"You know my name?" Raven asked, genuinely surprised.

"Yeah," said the boy, "you rented *She's All That* about two weeks ago. I sent you the late notice."

"The one with the smiley face?" asked Raven.

"Yeah, that was me. My name is Matthew," he said, holding out his hand.

Raven smiled as she took Matthew's hand. It was warm and strong—and when he smiled back at her, every muscle in her body seemed to melt.

"So, um, I'm here to pick up my little sister," said Matthew. "Why are you here?"

"I'm here—" Raven was about to say, "because this is Bayside Junior High, and I, like, *go to school* here." But just in time, she stopped herself.

Obviously, Matthew thought she was in high school. And Raven wanted him to *keep* thinking that.

"I'm here, I'm here . . ." repeated Raven, thinking fast. "You know, to pick up my little brother, Eddie." She pointed to her other best friend Eddie Thomas, who had just walked by.

"Eddie!" she called, shaking her finger. "Mom told me to give you a bath before dinner."

"Say what?" asked Eddie.

Raven quickly turned to Chelsea, "You go make sure he doesn't wander off."

Chelsea nodded, racing up to Eddie and

ushering him away before he could blow Raven's cover.

"So, Raven, I know we just sort of met," said Matthew, flashing his killer smile again, "but would you like to do something with me Friday night around eight?"

Raven hesitated. All the magazines said you should never accept a last-minute date with a guy.

"Wait. I don't know, Matthew," said Raven. "It's kind of short notice."

She had to show Matthew that she was a girl who made dates on her own terms. She wasn't desperate—no way, not Raven Baxter.

"Eight-*fifteen*?" she quickly suggested.

Matthew agreed, and after they said goodbye, Raven rushed off to find Chelsea.

"I have a date Friday night!" squealed Raven when she met up with her friend. "And he's seventeen."

Chelsea shook her head. She hated to burst her best friend's bliss bubble, but she knew how strict Mr. and Mrs. Baxter were.

"Rae, your parents are not gonna let you go out with a seventeen-year-old—" Chelsea stopped as she realized something. "Wait, Rae, that's your vision. Your parents are gonna say, 'no.'"

"No, no, no," said Raven. "See, that's only the first 'no.' The trick is you keep asking, and asking, and asking—"

Later that afternoon, Raven did keep asking, and asking, and asking if she could go out on a date Friday night.

Her parents were about to leave the house. But Raven was sure if she just kept hammering, she could pound that stubborn parental wall to dust.

Their final answer came before they left: "No, no, and no!"

Raven was stunned. Not only had they refused to budge, they'd even turned her down *in unison*, just like her vision.

"But can't we even talk about it—?" Raven complained.

Slam!

The door shut right in her face.

A moment later, her dad cracked the door and sheepishly peeked back through.

"I'm sorry, that was rude," he said. "Now where was I again? Oh, yeah. *No!*"

This time the door shut for good

Get Cheetah Power!

TV G
Bonus Material
Not Rated

Now on DVD and Video

Distributed by Buena Vista Home Entertainment, Inc., Burbank, California 91521. © Disney

Wake up.
Go to school.
Save the world.

The magic of friendship